AJAX PENUMBRA 1969

AJAX PENUMBRA 1969

ROBIN SLOAN

ATLANTIC BOOKS
London

First published in the United States of America in 2013 by
Farrar, Straus and Giroux, New York.

Published in Great Britain in 2014 by Atlantic Books, an imprint of
Atlantic Books Ltd.

10 9 8 7 6 5 4 3 2 1

A CIP catalogue record for this book is available from the British Library.

Hardback ISBN: 978 1 78239 517 1
E-Book ISBN: 978 1 78239 446 4

Printed in Italy by Grafica Veneta S.p.A.

CONTENTS

A 24-HOUR BOOKSTORE

A VISITOR WALKS THE city, searching. He has a list: libraries and bookstores, museums and archives. He descends into the bowels of the *San Francisco Chronicle*, follows a sullen clerk to the morgue's oldest files. There, the newsprint is brittle to the touch. He handles it carefully but confidently, his fingers trained for the task, but the *Chronicle* is too young. He does not find the name he is looking for.

The visitor canvasses Chinatown, learns to say *Bookstore?* in Cantonese: *Shu diàn?* He braves the haze of Haight Street, speaks to a long-haired man selling books on a blanket in Golden Gate Park. He crosses the bay to Cody's and Cal, ventures south to Kepler's and Stanford. He inquires at City Lights, but the man behind the register, whose name is Shig, shakes his head. "Never heard of him, man. Never heard of him." He sells the visitor a copy of "Howl" instead.

It is 1969, and San Francisco is under construction. The great central artery of Market Street is a trench. South of there, whole blocks have been knocked down and scraped clean; a fence is festooned with signs that proclaim it the YERBA BUENA GARDENS, though there is not a single plant or tree in evidence. To the north, the visitor passes a construction site where a wide ziggurat reaches for the sky and a placard promises THE FUTURE SITE OF THE TRANSAMERICA PYRAMID above a fine-lined rendering of a shining spear.

The visitor walks the city, disappointed. There is no place left to go; his list is folded and finished. He hikes to the Golden Gate Bridge, because he knows his parents will ask him about it. A quarter of the way across, he turns back. He expected a view of the city, but the bay is filled with fog, and his short-sleeved shirt is flapping in the frigid wind.

The visitor walks back to his hotel, going slowly, wallowing in his failure. In the morning, he will buy a train ticket home. He walks along the water for a while, then cuts into the city. He follows the border between North Beach and Chinatown, and there, wedged between an Italian restaurant and a Chinese pharmacy, he finds a bookstore.

Inside the restaurant, the chairs are all turned up on red-checked tablecloths. The pharmacy stands shadowed, doors drawn tight with dark loops of chain. The whole street is sleeping; it is nearly midnight. The bookstore, though, is wide awake.

He hears it before he sees it: the murmur of conversation, the tinny swirl of a song. The sound swells as the bookstore's door swings open and bodies tumble out into the street. The bodies are young, trailing long hair and loose fabric. The visitor hears the *flick* of a lighter, sees a leaping spark. The bodies pass something around, sighing and exhaling long plumes that merge with the fog. The visitor hangs back, watching. They pass the something around again, then fling it out into the street and go back inside.

He draws closer. The front of the store is all windows, top to bottom, square panes set into a grid of iron, entirely fogged over. Inside, it looks like a party in progress. He sees faces and hands, dark mops of hair, all made Impressionistic by the foggy glass. The song is one he has heard elsewhere in the city; something popular.

He pushes the door and a wave of yeasty warmth washes over him. Somewhere above, a bell tinkles brightly, announcing him, but no one notices. He cannot get the door entirely open; it bumps up against someone's back, someone's loose jacket covered with a constellation of patches. The visitor squeezes in sideways, muttering a quiet apology, but the jacket-wearer doesn't notice; he is engrossed in conversation with a woman clutching a portable radio, the source of the swirling song.

The bookstore is tiny: tall and narrow. From his position near the corner, the visitor surveys the space and decides that there are fewer customers here than at City Lights, probably less than two dozen—it's just that they are all squashed into a fraction of the floor space.

The small-but-concentrated crowd wraps itself around

several low tables, each sprouting a small handwritten sign, like POETRY and SCIENCE FICTION and AS SEEN IN THE *WHOLE EARTH* CATALOG. Some in the crowd are browsing the books; two bushy-bearded men pick at the CINEMA table, arguing and gesticulating. Others are reading outright; a woman in a green dress stands in place, mesmerized by a *Fantastic Four* comic book. Mostly, though, the crowd is paying attention to itself: talking, nodding, laughing, flirting, lifting hair from eyes, tucking it back behind ears. Everyone has long hair, and the visitor feels suddenly self-conscious about his number 3 buzz.

He snakes his way through the crowd, heading for the cash register, trying not to touch anyone. Hygiene levels range widely. Voices echo on the bare floorboards, and he picks up scraps of conversation:

"… a trip, you know …"

"… up in Marin …"

"… at the Led Zep …"

"… like, dog food …"

There is more to the bookstore. Beyond the low tables, dominating the back half of the store, there are shelves that stretch taller and disappear into the darkness above. Ladders extend perilously up into the gloom. The heavy denizens of those shelves look altogether more serious than the books up front, and the crowd seems to leave them alone—although it is possible, the visitor supposes, that some furtive activity is taking place in the deepest shadows.

He feels profoundly uncomfortable. He wants to turn

around and leave. But … this is a bookstore. It might hold some clue.

When the visitor reaches the cash register, he finds the clerk arguing with a customer. The figures contrast sharply: two different decades facing off across a wide, heavy desk. The customer is a bendy twig of a man with stringy hair tied into a ponytail; the clerk is a sturdy plank with thick arms that stretch the wales of his sweater. He has a neat mustache under dark hair slicked back from his brow; he looks less like a bookstore clerk and more like a sailor.

"The restroom is for customers," the clerk insists.

"I bought a book last week, man," the customer protests.

"Is that so? I have no doubt that you *read* a book last week—oh, I saw you doing it—but as for *purchasing* …" The clerk hauls out a fat leather-bound tome, flips deftly through its pages. "No, I'm afraid I don't see anything here…. What's your name again?"

The customer smiles beatifically. "Coyote."

"Coyote, of course…. No, I don't see any Coyote here. I see a Starchild … a Frodo … but no Coyote."

"Starchild, yeah! That's my *last* name. Come on, man. I gotta take a whiz." The customer—Coyote … Starchild?—bounces on his heels.

The clerk clenches his jaw. He produces a skeleton key with a long gray tassel. "Be quick about it." The customer snatches the key and disappears between the tall shelves; as he goes, two others fall into step alongside him.

"No loitering!" the clerk calls after them. "No …" He

sighs, then snaps his head around to face the visitor. "Well? What?"

"Ah. Hello." The visitor smiles. "I am looking for a book."

The clerk pauses. Recalibrates. "Really?" His jaw seems to unclench.

"Yes. Or rather, I mean that I am looking for a *particular* book."

"Marcus!" a voice calls out. The clerk's gaze lifts. The woman with the portable radio is hoisting a book up above the crowd, jabbing a finger at its cover: *Naked Came the Stranger*. "*Mar*-cus! You been reading this while nobody's around, right?"

The clerk frowns, and does not favor her with a reply, but bounces a fist on the surface of the desk and mutters, to no one in particular, "I don't know why he would stock anything so tawdry…"

"A particular book," the visitor prods gently.

The clerk's gaze snaps back. He presses his mouth into a tight line; something well short of a smile. "Of course. What's the title?"

The visitor says it slowly, enunciating clearly: "The *Techne Tycheon*. That's *T-E-C-H—*"

"Yes, *techne*, I know. And with *tycheon* … that would be 'the craft of fortune,' correct?"

"Exactly so!" the visitor exclaims.

"*Mar-cus!*" the woman's voice calls again. This time, the clerk ignores her entirely.

"Contrary to however it might appear," he says flatly,

"this *is* a place of scholarly inquiry." He retrieves an oblong book, wider than it is tall. "I don't recognize that title, but let me double-check." He flips through the pages, revealing a gridded ledger—a kind of catalog. "Nothing under *T* … What's the author's name?"

The visitor shakes his head. "It is a very old volume. I only have the title. But I know it was here, in San Francisco, at a bookstore managed by a certain … Well, it is a somewhat complicated story."

The clerk's eyes narrow, not with suspicion, but with deep interest. He sets the catalog aside. "Tell me."

"It is—ah." The visitor turns, expecting to see customers queuing behind him; there is no one. He turns back to the clerk. "It will take some time."

"It's a twenty-four-hour bookstore," the clerk says. He smiles almost ruefully. "We've got nothing but time."

"I should start at the beginning."

"You should start with the basics." The clerk settles back on his stool, crosses his arms. "What's your name, friend?"

"Oh. Yes, of course. My name is Ajax Penumbra."

AJAX PENUMBRA!

HOW DO YOU get a name like Ajax Penumbra? Like this: You are conceived by Pablo and Maria Penumbra, who flee Spain only months before a great civil war erupts. Your father carries a trunk full of books; your mother carries you.

You are born in England. From Maria, a schoolteacher, you get your barking laugh, your jangling grin. From Pablo, a perpetually struggling poet, you get your height and your name, like the Greek hero. In disposition, it turns out that you are perhaps more like Ajax's rival Odysseus, and of course your father considered that name, too, but Maria exercised her veto power. A boy named Odysseus Penumbra, she said, would not survive the seventh grade.

You spend your early years in transit: from England to Canada to America. Specifically, to Galesburg, Illinois, where Maria takes a post at a high school, and where she rises, in time, to the rank of principal. Pablo founds a literary journal titled *Migraciones.* It accumulates, over the whole course of your childhood, a total of seventy-three subscribers.

Your parents are weirdos, in the best possible way. They do not celebrate birthdays; never in your life have you received a present on the tenth of December. Instead, you are given books on the days that their authors were born. It will be January 27, and a package will be waiting at the foot of the stairs, wrapped in bright paper. The note: "To my darling boy, on the occasion of Lewis Carroll's 93rd birthday." *Through the Looking-Glass, and What Alice Found There.*

AJAX PENUMBRA. At tiny Galvanic College, known as the Harvard of Northwestern Illinois, your student ID bears your name in monospaced caps and, alongside it, your mug shot, showing a creature made entirely of neck, ears, and teeth. Your big goofy grin. Looking at it, you wish you had restrained yourself. Tried to look more serious.

Standing before you and all the rest of the incoming freshmen, Galvanic's president proudly declares that your dorm room assignments are, for the first time, the result of a *computerized process.* At first, it appears that the computer has made a grievous error. Your roommate, Claude Novak, is a fast-talking Chicagoan; you are a small-town introvert. He is short and intense; you are tall and reserved. He smokes; you skulk. Claude seems out of place at this college set amidst cornfields; you fit right in with the pale stalks.

But as you unpack on that first day, the computer's logic is revealed: both of you have loaded your trunks primarily with books, relegating nice-to-haves like pants and shoes to the crevices between volumes. On that first day, you stand shoulder to shoulder, heads tilted to the side, scanning your combined collection on the rickety dorm room bookcase. Your contribution is heavy on Shakespeare, Dante, Homer—your father's influence. Claude, by contrast, has brought nothing but science fiction. The covers show sleek spacecraft, sparking humanoid robots, and green-skinned Martian babes.

You stay up all night reading.

Claude came for the computer. Galvanic possesses one of the most powerful machines in the Midwest, a recent and somewhat eccentric gift from a rich alumnus, yet the college's faculty and students combined number less than three thousand. Claude did the math—divided processor cycles by campus population—and decided that Galvanic, not the University of Illinois, would be his best shot at computer time.

He spends most days, and many nights, down in the second subbasement of McDonald Hall, where the great hulking machine is rumored to reside. Claude invites you to visit. You descend two flights of stairs and creep down the cool, shadowed hallway. The door ahead is propped open, and from inside, you feel an icy chill. The plaque beside the door reads B3, but a sign taped below, written in Claude's squiggly handwriting, proclaims it THE FOUNDATION.

Inside, you meet a computer face-to-face for the first time. It is not a great elephantine contraption, as you expected, but instead a cluster of tall boxes, all with the look of super-modern kitchen appliances, clad in smooth panels that flash silvery gray and flame red. Spools of tape, as big around as dinner plates, spin slowly behind glass windows. Everything is marked with the same blocky logo: IBM.

Something—possibly one of the appliances—is making the room very, very cold. Claude sits at a tiny table in the center of the cluster; he is bundled up, wearing a ski mask and a winter jacket.

"Hey, buddy!" he calls out, rolling his mask up around his head. The scene is strange, but really no stranger than the basic premise of your roommate sitting here, using a computer.

Using a computer is just not a thing that a person does.

Claude spins a plastic chair around, places it alongside his at the table. "You're just in time." He is sorting a thick stack of punch cards, waxy and yellowish, all with the same bold heading: DO NOT FOLD, SPINDLE, OR MUTILATE. You sit, rubbing your arms against the cold.

Claude slots the cards into a small bin, then presses stubby buttons in a short, confident sequence. The cards begin to disappear; the computer gobbles them up, one by one, clacking and purring.

You ask: "W-what exactly … is it doing?"

"Navier-Stokes equations, mostly. Oh, sorry, you mean— Right. The computer reads the cards, follows the instructions, and I get answers … there." He points to a printer loaded with a fat cylinder of paper. It has already disgorged several yards of answers, now pooled on the cement floor.

"And what will those answers … reveal?"

"I'm working on weather. That's the hot topic right now in computer science … climate models, fallout diffusion, et cetera. Sooo, I feed in today's observed temperatures, wind speeds, et cetera … I have to normalize the grid points first, of course … and then I supply my prediction model—that's where the Navier-Stokes equations come into play"—he is talking very quickly and very excitedly—"aaand I find out if it's going to rain tomorrow." He taps his finger the table: *tap, tap tap tap*. "In Moscow."

You visit room B3 many times after that, always with your winter jacket. The computer makes you nervous; when Claude invites you to press the stubby buttons yourself, you demur. But you watch, and you listen as he talks—quickly, excitedly—about all the problems that an even more powerful computer will be able to solve.

"Economic projections," he says. "Traffic simulations. Chess!"

You arrive at Galvanic as an English major, but over the course of your first semester, you learn that the college offers a more specialized program for students with more … specialized interests. Its courses are not listed in the catalog, at least not plainly. Instead, they are camouflaged among the

English department's offerings: prime-numbered, with titles so stultifying—such as English 103, *Sentence Diagrams*—that no sane student would ever enroll without a very good reason.

The course meets in the college's great gray gargoyle-encrusted library, up on the top floor, where arrowslit windows look out across the cornfields, reluctant to admit too much light. Your instructor is a burly, frog-throated man named Langston Armitage. He is, he explains, the head of the Occult Literature department. The other students all nod eagerly, but you are confused. You signed up because you legitimately enjoy diagramming sentences.

On the first day of your second semester, you walk to the registrar's office and switch your major.

That spring, in the first session of English 211, *The History of the Index*—actually Occult Lit 211, *Dangerous Books*—Armitage explains that Galvanic's library contains more one-of-a-kind, untranslatable, and/or inexplicable volumes than any other collection on earth. In the second session, he sends you down into the stacks. There are books made from silver and bone. There are books with blood on their pages, figuratively and literally. There are books made of feathers; books cloaked in jade; books that ring like bells when you pull them off the shelf; books that glow in the dark.

Claude Novak graduates in just three years. On a cool summer morning, you walk with him to Galvanic's little train station, each of you gripping one end of his trunk, weighed down with science fiction. He is bound for California, where he will join Stanford's graduate program in computer science—one of the country's first. Before the train arrives, he plucks a book out of the trunk and presents it to you. The cover shows a pale, swirling galaxy. It is Isaac Asimov's *Foundation*; Claude has spoken of this one often.

You confirm: "Scientists predict the future?"

"Psychohistorians," he says lightly. "And this one's not science fiction, buddy. Not anymore. It's going to be real."

When the train arrives, you shake Claude's hand, and then you grow solemn. "I am grateful to the computerized process that matched us," you tell your erstwhile roommate. "I hope you will write algorithms of your own that produce such happy results."

Claude laughs. "Me, too, buddy. Me, too. Good luck in the library."

Books of silver; books of bone; and yet the strangest thing you see in all your years at Galvanic is a boy in a ski mask, sitting in a basement, using a computer.

A year later, when you are preparing to graduate, Langston Armitage invites you into his aerie on the top floor of the library. His single narrow window is covered with a strip of paisley wallpaper, but the sunlight still presses through, giving everything in the office a greenish cast. Including Armitage.

"I would like to invite you to join the library staff," he croaks.

You have worked at the library for three summers, shelving and reshelving books, auditing and updating the card catalog, and although you love the place, this does not sound like an exciting next step. It must show on your face, because Armitage elaborates:

"No, my boy. I mean the *acquisitions* staff."

Four years of Occult Lit classes have served as more-or-less continuous propaganda for the Galvanic College Library acquisitions staff. They are the long arm of the library, and the wellspring of its bibliographic wealth. You see them sometimes on the library's upper floors, consulting with one another in the shadows, speaking quietly in strange languages, rubbing thoughtfully at strange scars.

That summer, you become an Apprentice Acquisitions Officer, and begin what is a graduate program in all but degree. You are paid to read the classics, and also books that *would* be classics if any library other than Galvanic's possessed them. You are paid to learn languages: Greek and Latin, certainly, but older ones, too—Aramaic and Sanskrit and Proto-Phoenician, which might have been the language of Atlantis.

Up in Galesburg, your mother retires, and the marching band plays a farewell concert on your old front lawn. Your father gets sick, spends a month in the hospital, gets better—though his voice is always different after that. Softer. He founds a new journal, *Interrupciones*.

Things go more slowly than you had, perhaps, expected. Years pass before Langston Armitage judges you ready for your first assignment. On that day, he calls you into his office, promotes you to the post of Junior Acquisitions Officer, and gives you your assignment: a book known as the *Techne Tycheon*.

You translate from Greek: "The art, or craft, of fortune."

"Very good. It has a long history—here." He pulls an overstuffed folder out of its place midway down the tower on his desk; several others slide out with it and scatter their contents across the floor. "This"—he taps the folder—"is the work of another acquisitions officer, Jack Brindle. You will find that the trail runs cold circa 1657."

"What happened to Brindle?"

"Died in Macau. Very mysterious. In any case—1657. You'll pick it up from there."

You learn that the *Tycheon*—as it is more casually known to the approximately three people alive who care about its existence—did not enjoy a large print run, but the few copies that ever existed made quite an impression. It is, apparently, a book of prophecy, and Brindle's file is full of suggestive scraps. In 1511, a merchant in Liverpool extolls its virtues. Almost a century later, in 1601, a fortune-teller in London cannot work without it. The fortune-teller's apprentice praises the *Tycheon* just as effusively, but apparently misses an important prediction; he is murdered in 1657. The trail goes red, and cold. Your quest begins. You ride the train to Urbana, Chicago, East Lansing, and Ann Arbor. In university libraries and antiquarian bookstores, you collect fragments, grasp at footnotes, and, over time, assemble an overstuffed file of your own. It is not any more useful than Brindle's. You fling letters of inquiry far and wide, but when the replies come, they carry only regrets.

You begin to suspect that the *Tycheon* might simply be lost. You confess as much to Langston Armitage, and he reminds you that your colleague Carol Janssen recently recovered the six-hundred-year-old Incan *Book of Dreams*. "It was composed entirely from knotted string, my boy," he croaks, "and they had taken it apart to make sweaters." He says it again, for emphasis: "It was in … the villagers' … *sweaters*."

You keep at it. You trace receipts and track manifests. And then: a breakthrough.

In the papers of a New York surgeon and bibliophile named Floyd Deckle, there is a letter from a friend, Dr. Victor Potente, sent from San Francisco, dated September 1861. Potente writes:

> And here, no bookseller is so well stocked as the great William Gray, boasting first editions of Galen and Vesalius, as well as another volume less scientific, but no less noteworthy: a book of prophecy! Rest assured, Floyd, I pressed the clerk to reveal its contents, but he refused, claiming that special training is required to interpret its fell omens. I offered, as substitute, my surgical *education—surely, I said, I have learned to read certain dark signs—but the clerk, a*

Mr. Fang, only shook his head, and to its place of safekeeping he returned the volume, which bore the title—The craft of fortune.

Your eyes widen. You copy the name. *William Gray*. Copy it twice. You sprint through the stacks, clamber up the stairs, trip on your own feet, fall on your hands. On the top floor, you pound on Langston Armitage's door—lungs heaving, palms stinging—and wait for his croaked command: "Enter!"

Armitage listens intently as you reveal your discovery: a new reference, the most contemporaneous by two centuries! The name of the bookseller: William Gray of San Francisco! The missing link!

Armitage's lips pull into a tight line. "San Francisco," he croaks. You nod. Armitage nods back. Then he lifts one stubby arm into an operatic curve, and in a vibrating baritone he sings: "If you're gooo-ing … to Saaan Fraaan-cisco …" He breaks off. Casts a glance up at your buzz cut. Stabs a finger. "Not much to hold the flowers up there, Ajax."

You exhale. Gather yourself. "So I should go west?"

"My boy! You should already be gone."

FRIEDRICH & FANG

PENUMBRA DOES NOT tell the clerk all of this, but he does tell him more than is strictly necessary to describe the object of his quest. The clerk listens intently, his eyebrows lowered in concentration, the broad field of his forehead furrowed. More longhairs approach the desk to inquire about the bathroom key. The clerk surrenders it silently, without protest. Almost without looking.

Penumbra finishes his tale with the name of the San Francisco bookseller. The clerk is quiet, thinking.

"Well," he says at last. "I don't know about any William Gray."

"I have grown accustomed to that reply. It is not—"

The clerk holds up a hand. "Wait. We'll ask Mo."

"Mo?"

The front door crashes open and the bell above clatters harshly. Penumbra turns to watch as an unseen presence charges through the crowd, its passage marked by a ripple of greetings:

"Hey, Mo."

"Mo!"

"How's it hanging, Mo?"

"Mo, my main man!"

The sea of longhairs parts, and there, standing barely five feet tall, gleamingly bald, is a man who can only be Mohammed Al-Asmari. Round-rimmed glasses rest on the sharp hook of his nose. He wears a snug jacket, dark and shiny, with a neat Nehru collar. He turns to address the store:

"Out! All of you!" He waves his hands in a shooing motion. "Go home! Go to sleep!"

There is no reaction whatsoever. The song plays on; the crowd laughs and flirts unimpeded. When the store's proprietor turns to face the wide desk again, he is smiling, lighting up the network of deep creases across his face. "A healthy crowd tonight, Mr. Corvina."

The clerk—Corvina—frowns. "They've bought two books between them, Mo."

"Oh, that's fine," Mo says, waving a hand. "This business is all about relationships. We wait for the right moment. Observe."

He turns, raises his voice again: "You there! Felix, isn't it? You've been reading that book for three nights straight—buy it already!" His target shouts a good-natured protest, mimes empty pockets. Mo calls back: "Nonsense! Pass a hat around. You can raise three dollars from this band of hooligans."

There is a light chorus of jeers. Mo turns back, still smiling. "And here?" He peers up at Penumbra. "A new face?"

"A more serious customer," Corvina says approvingly. "Mohammed Al-Asmari, meet Ajax Penumbra."

"Ajax!" Mo repeats. He looks him up and down. "Your parents must have had high expectations."

"They—well. My father is a poet." Penumbra extends a hand. "It is a pleasure to meet you, Mr. Al-Asmari."

"Please! I beg you. Call me Mo." He clasps Penumbra's hand with both of his together. "Welcome, welcome to the 24-Hour Bookstore. I don't suppose you read about us in *Rolling Stone*? …"

"Ah—no. I do not—"

Corvina interjects: "He's looking for a very particular book, Mo."

"As are we all, Mr. Corvina, as are we all. Most don't realize it yet. So on that count, our friend Ajax Penumbra is ahead."

"It is a very old book," Penumbra says. "I have traced the most contemporaneous reference to this city, to a bookstore that no longer exists. I came here with the hope that some rumor of the volume's passage might persist among booksellers such as yourself."

Mo trots around to the back of the desk, shoos Corvina from the stool, hoists himself up to take his place. "I see the 'Howl' in your back pocket, Mr. Penumbra"—he jabs a finger down from his perch—"so I know you visited our upstart competitor before venturing here. But they could not assist you, could they? No, of course not. Here, we have a longer memory. But tell me, tell me—what do you seek?"

Penumbra repeats his story. Midway through, a fuzzy-chinned young man approaches the desk with a battered copy of *Dune* and a motley handful of coins. Mo waves him away. "Oh, just take it, Felix. Spend the money on a haircut."

Penumbra finishes. He and Corvina both watch Mo expectantly, waiting for some reaction.

"William Gray." Mo says it slowly. "Well. This is very interesting indeed."

Penumbra brightens. "You have heard of him?"

"I know the name," Mo says. Four simple words, but they send a thrill down Penumbra's spine. "And I'll tell you how," Mo continues. He turns to his clerk. "Listen closely, Mr. Corvina. This will be of some interest to you, as well."

The store has grown quieter; the woman with the portable radio has departed. Mo laces his fingers together and rests his chin there. "To begin, Mr. Penumbra—you have it half right."

Penumbra raises an eyebrow at that. "Which half, precisely?"

Mo is silent. Drawing it out. Then he says: "William Gray wasn't a man. The *William Gray* was a ship."

"That is not possible," Penumbra says, shaking his head. "I have a specific reference to a bookstore."

Mo regards him from behind the curl of his knuckles. "How much do you know about the ground upon which you stand?"

"About this city? I admit that I am no native, but I have found the works of Herb Caen most—"

Mo snorts. "Come with me. Both of you." He hops down from the stool and trots toward the front door. To the fuzzy-chinned *Dune* reader, he calls: "Felix! Watch the store!"

Outside, thin whips of fog are snapping across the street. Mo shivers and straightens his collar, tugs it up higher. "Come along," he says, trotting down the sidewalk, following the slope toward the bay. His shadow spins under the streetlamps. Penumbra and Corvina obey, and they all walk in silence for several blocks. The fog closes in; the bookstore behind them is just a ghostly glimmer.

"Here." Mo stops suddenly. "This is San Francisco."

Penumbra gives him a puzzled look.

"And this—" Mo hops one step forward. "—is the bay. Or it was, before they filled it in. I stand upon the *new* San Francisco. Landfill."

Corvina bends down close to the ground, as if he might detect some difference. The concrete is cold and smooth.

"Mainly, it's rubble from 1906, the great earthquake and fire," Mo says. "But there are other things down there, too. There are ships."

"Ships," Penumbra repeats.

"It was 1849. Ships were sailing into this city every day, every one of them loaded with would-be prospectors. They disembarked—some of them leaping into the water for a head start—and they ran for the goldfields. Well, now. These ships' crews had just spent the whole passage listening to those lunatics rave, and now they didn't want to be left behind. They thought their fortunes were waiting in those fields, too! So they abandoned ship, every one of them. Even the captains."

Corvina frowns. "They abandoned them entirely?"

"Entirely and without hesitation, Mr. Corvina. There were globs of gold waiting to be gathered up like so many fallen apples!—or so they thought. In any case, without captain or crew, the ships went to the highest bidder. They stayed put, mostly, and they were repurposed—truly, put to *every* purpose. They had street addresses! They became storehouses. Boardinghouses. Brothels. Prisons."

Realization dawns across Penumbra's face. "Bookstores."

"Just one. That was the *William Gray*."

"I had it all wrong," Penumbra moans. He claps his palm to his forehead, digs his fingers into his hair. "I was looking for the wrong thing entirely."

Mo is thoughtful, gazing out toward the water. "Yes, the *William Gray* became a bookstore, the first this city ever had. It was established by two men, a Mr. Friedrich and a Mr. Fang." Corvina perks up at the name, and seems ready to say something, but Mo continues: "They were fast friends. Friedrich came from Germany. Fang was born here, in San Francisco. Oh, yes, Mr. Corvina—" Here, he looks pointedly at his clerk. "—Mr. Fang had a partner. But only for a time."

Penumbra glances at Corvina, puzzled. The clerk looks confused, as well. Mo continues:

"For a decade, their joint venture bobbed in the bay, a beacon of erudition in an otherwise fairly depraved environment. But, I am sorry to report that Mr. Friedrich's interest … waned. The market for real estate in San Francisco was no saner in his day than ours, and an *innovation* was sweeping the city. Speculators would acquire so-called water plots—little bits of the bay, you see?—and fill them in. It was alchemy! Instant waterfront property. And one method—oh, it would be funny, if it weren't so sad—one particularly expeditious method was … to simply sink a ship."

"No!" Penumbra bleats. "Surely, not the *William Gray*? …"

"One morning—Ah, I can hardly imagine it. It was a singular betrayal, not just of Mr. Fang, but of all those … ah." Mo shakes his head. The streetlamp above him shines down harshly, casting fine shadows, making webs of his wrinkled cheeks. "One morning, Mr. Fang arrived at his great floating bookstore on Beale Street, only to find that it no longer floated. Friedrich had scuttled the ship. Only the tip of the mast poked up out of the water."

Penumbra gapes. "What did Fang do?"

"Why, he did what any self-respecting bookseller would do, Mr. Penumbra." There is a dark twinkle in Mo's eye. "He dived!"

Penumbra barks a single great laugh. "Ha! He did not."

"He did!" Mo insisted. "He dived, and dived, and dived

again. He retrieved what he could. In the end, only a few volumes could be dried and recopied. And those—" Again, he looks at Corvina. "—form the core of our collection even today."

"I didn't know Fang was the first," Corvina says.

"Oh, yes. He reestablished the store in our present location. We have him to blame for the odd dimensions, Mr. Corvina, and him to thank for the bell above the door."

"Did he save the *Techne Tycheon*?" Penumbra asks, almost frantic. His assignment is flashing before his eyes. "Do you still possess a book with that title?"

"That would be ... the 'craft of fortune'—do I have it right?"

Penumbra nods. San Francisco is, apparently, a good town for Greek.

Mo pauses, consulting his mental inventory. "I'm sorry, Mr. Penumbra—but I am quite sure that we do not."

"It was aboard the *William Gray*," Penumbra insists. "I have proof."

"Then it is gone. That ship was lost. And now—" Mo lifts his hands to encompass the sidewalk, the street, the storefronts—the whole dark tableau, sliding down toward the bay. "And now, a great city has risen over it."

PSYCHOHISTORIAN

He walks the city, dispirited. It is something, he tells himself, to have determined the fate of the *William Gray* and the book he sought there. But it is still a failure. His first assignment as a Junior Acquisitions Officer, and it came to nothing.

Carol Janssen found the *Book of Dreams* in a remote Peruvian village. Another acquisitions officer, Julian Lemire, pulled the diary of Nebuchadnezzar II out of an active volcano. Langston Armitage himself has traveled to Antarctica twice. Now, Penumbra has come so close to his own prize, and yet it is beyond his reach. A whole city blocks his way.

He turns now to another task, one that he will not leave without attempting. At the library, in a thick Palo Alto phone book, he finds NOVAK, CLAUDE CASIMIR. His old roommate went to Stanford and he never left.

The Peninsula Commute train takes him chugging through a loose necklace of towns: San Mateo, Hillsdale, San Carlos, Redwood City, Menlo Park, and finally, Palo Alto.

Traveling up and down the peninsula, Penumbra has come to the conclusion that San Francisco is not actually part of California. The city is pale and windswept; Palo Alto is green and still, with the scent of eucalyptus strong in the air. The sky here is pearlescent blue, not platinum gray. Penumbra lifts his face to the generous sun and wonders: Why did I wait so long to visit my old roommate here?

Claude Novak's house is a small stucco box with a red-tile roof, the lawn dry and brown beneath a tree that rises to dwarf the house utterly. It is, Penumbra realizes, a redwood. Claude lives beneath a redwood tree.

Inside, there is no furniture. Everything sits on the floor, on the green shag carpet. Thick pads of graph paper are stacked in squat towers; pencils and pens are collected in coffee cups, or poking out of the carpet. There are piles of books with intimidating titles: *Finite State Machines*, *Modern Matrix Algebra*, *Detours in Hilbert Space*. Claude's other library has grown, too. It is gathered in a long block, forming a sort of low wall around the brown-tiled kitchen. Creased paperback spines show the authors' names in bold capitals: ASIMOV BRADBURY CLARKE DEL REY ... A fuzzy gray cat skulks behind the science fiction and mewls at the intruder.

"Make yourself comfortable," Claude says. He plops

down on the floor, where there is also a pizza box, a *San Jose Mercury News*, a single wilted plant, and, in the center of the room, roughly where a dining table should sit, rising between two precarious heaps of books and binders …

"Claude, is that a computer?"

He nods. "I built it myself." If the machine at Galvanic was sleek and stylish, this one is rough-hewn and functional—a plywood box with a loose, soapbox-derby look. It is much smaller, too: a piece of luggage, not a kitchen appliance. The top panel has been pulled back, and the computer's guts poke out from inside: long boards studded with electronic components that glint like tiny stones and shells.

"To put this in perspective," Claude says, "it's about one-fourth the size of that old IBM, but twice as powerful."

The computer is running; lights flutter and flow across the front panel. There is a keyboard and a boxy green and black monitor showing fuzzy characters. Penumbra gazes at it, mesmerized. Claude built this himself.

Building a computer is just not a thing that a person does.

"How are you?" Claude asks. "I mean—how's *life*?"

Penumbra sits, and he tells him everything. He tells him about his job at the library, the *Techne Tycheon*, his odyssey in San Francisco, the *William Gray*.

"That's fantastic," Claude says. "It suits you, buddy. You've found your calling. Cigarette?"

Penumbra demurs and watches his old roommate light one on his own.

"A ship buried beneath the city," Claude says. "Heavy."

He exhales slowly and taps his cigarette into an ashtray that says STAR TREK across the side.

"It is an unfortunate conclusion," Penumbra admits, "but it is, at least, a conclusion. Better to know the truth, I think, than—"

"Wait," Claude says suddenly. He taps his finger on the ashtray. *Tap, tap tap tap*. "BART. Yes. I worked on the projections. Ridership, regional uptake, route scenarios, et cetera. I have the … hold on …" He is up on his feet, bent over, rummaging through one of his piles. Folders are sliding tectonically down onto the carpet. The cat yowls. "It's in here somewhere … system map, timetables, et cetera … aha!" He lifts a sheaf of paper triumphantly. "BART!"

"Who is … Bart?"

"BART, buddy. *B-A-R-T*, Bay Area Rapid Transit. The train system, you know? They're building it now. You must have seen it … the whole city is torn to hell."

"Of course. BART."

"Now … look at this." Claude unfolds the sheaf, showing a geometric approximation of the Bay Area. There's the long peninsula, the blocky knob of the city, and across the bay, the crenellated curve of Oakland and Berkeley. The contours are drawn in plain black and white, but laid across the landscape there is a bundle of colored lines: red, yellow, blue, and green. Claude points to the bundle where it cuts through San Francisco. "They're digging this right now. I mean, *right* now."

"And you worked on this? Planning it?"

"Like I said, ridership projections. Different scenarios. High gas prices, low gas prices, thermonuclear war, et cetera."

"Claude." Penumbra beams. "You are a psychohistorian after all."

"Ha! You read *Foundation.* I wish the people I work with appreciated that .... Not too many Asimov fans in my department. Anyway, the point is, I hear plenty about the excavation. They're finding things. Old underground speakeasies ... basements people didn't know they had."

Penumbra's eyes go wide. "And ships?"

"Maybe, maybe not. All I can tell you is that this tunnel—" He points to the rainbow bundle where it crosses a point labeled EMBARCADERO. "—runs straight through landfill. They have to go slow there ... dig carefully."

Penumbra's brain is buzzing. "How would I determine if the wreck of the *William Gray* lies in their path?"

"I can't help you there. I can tell you that two hundred fifty-eight thousand people are going to be riding this thing on January 1, 1975. But—ha—my model has nothing to say about sunken ships." He drags on his cigarette. "I thought the old stuff was your specialty, buddy."

Penumbra thinks of their rickety bookcase: his classics on one shelf, Claude's science fiction on the other. It is, he realizes, an image that would fit the cover of one of his old roommate's books: a ghostly shipwreck rising from below a futuristic city ....

He smiles. "You are right. I can manage this on my own."

The San Francisco Public Library is a pale marble fortress facing City Hall across a bleak promenade lined with palm trees. Inside, a grand central stairway is flanked by pale murals showing swaths of empty ocean, with wispy clouds floating at the upper edges. The effect is, Penumbra thinks, quite depressing.

He has been here once before, and he left in a foul mood after a full day of fruitless searching. Then, he was looking at birth certificates, deeds of sale, court records—the sources you consult when you are searching for a man with a business. This morning, he is looking for a ship with a street address.

He makes for the map room. It is narrow and crowded, dominated by tall brown filing cabinets with wide, flat drawers. The librarian, a woman in a flower-print dress, is bent over reading *Portnoy's Complaint*.

"I wish to see every map of San Francisco produced between 1849 and 1861," Penumbra declares.

She looks up, startled. "You want ... all of them?"

He wants all of them.

He has not yet purchased a train ticket home.

THE GIFT

He comes hustling into the bookstore before noon; the overnight crowd has not yet gathered. A pair of tourists browses the WHOLE EARTH table, speaking to one another quietly in German, gesturing up toward the tall shelves.

Penumbra plants his palms on the wide desk. He is out of breath; cheeks flushed; shirt askew. He has come running from the library. Corvina regards him with a raised eyebrow and the rumor of a smile. "Welcome back."

"I—*whew*. Oh, goodness." He takes a gulp of air. "I have a map!"

Penumbra produces his treasure. It shows a city with two coastlines. One, the modern coast, is drawn smoothly; the other, older coast is a wandering dotted line. The old coast bites deep into downtown, flooding whole neighborhoods. Along the dotted line, there is a dusting of neat numerals, and in the map's corner, there is a broad legend that matches numbers to names: *Cadmus*, *Canonicus*, *Euphemia* ... the

Martha Watson, the *Thomas Bennett*, the *Philip Hone* … and then, there it sits, along the angled cut of Market Street. There it rests, number 43, the *William Gray*, snuggled up against the dotted coast.

Corvina looks from the map to Penumbra; from Penumbra back to the map; up again. "You found this?"

"It was a simple matter once I knew—*whew*—where to look. And, I suppose, *why* to look." Penumbra drags a finger down Market Street. "This is the path of the BART tunnel. They are digging straight past the ship, Marcus."

Corvina nods once. "Take this to Mo."

At the back of the store, there are three doors. The first is ajar, and inside, Penumbra sees the detritus of a small break room: a table, two chairs, a lunch box. The next door is shut tight, and two small brass letters label it the WC; below them, a sign scrawled in jagged capitals reserves it FOR PAYING CUSTOMERS ONLY. Finally, there is a third door, also marked with two brass letters—but these letters spell MO.

The door is open, and behind it, stairs rise steeply into darkness. Penumbra pokes his head through and calls out: "Hello?" There is no reply. He begins the climb. From above, a spicy smell wafts down and tickles his nose.

He emerges at the top into a sprawling space, the walls hung with tapestries, all of them densely embroidered, some with metallic threads that shine in the low golden light. They show dancers in pointed shoes, musicians clutching curling horns, scribes wielding feather pens as tall as themselves. If the room has windows, the tapestries cover them. Penumbra's shoes thud quietly; the fabric muffles the sound and give the space an eerie sense of absorption. It feels a step removed from space and time.

"Mr. Al-Asmari?" Penumbra says tentatively.

There is a massive desk in the center of the room, twin to the one in the store below. On the desk, there sits a lamp, its light focused into a tight pool, and above the pool there floats a face, lit starkly from below.

"Mr. Penumbra," the face intones. It is Mo, but here, he is transformed. His glasses reflect lunar ovals of lamplight; the eyes behind them are obscured. "How many times must I beg you? Call me Mo."

"But you—"

"Please."

"Of course. Mo." It feels awkward on his lips. "I was just at the public library—I was doing some research, and—well, I found a map."

"Maps are good. I like maps. Can I offer you some coffee? My special blend." The spicy smell resolves: cardamom. There is a plume of steam rising from a pale cup on the desk, coiling up into the lamplight, glowing almost gold.

"Yes, please. Thank you."

Mo pours fragrant coffee from a filigreed pot swaddled in a purple cloth—altogether, a very classy thermos—and clinks the cup down under the lamp. "Sit. Sip. Enjoy."

Penumbra obeys. The coffee is very hot and very thick; it seems to coat his throat. He sees that Mo has been consulting a serious-looking book—clearly one of the volumes from the tall shelves. The pages are covered with Chinese characters.

Mo catches his gaze. "Ah! This is not the public library, Mr. Penumbra. These books are not for browsing." He snaps the cover shut. "Although I should confess that I have been doing some research of my own." He lifts the books to show Penumbra the spine. White letters, widely spaced, spell out FANG.

"Fang, as in the bookseller Fang?"

"Yes. The first of my predecessors. Mr. Friedrich would share that distinction, except of course that he sank his own ship and sent his partner scrambling for a new home. Mr. Fang found this building—did I tell you that? And Friedrich has been … erased from our records."

"What does Fang have to say there?" Penumbra asks, indicating the book.

Mo removes his glasses and rubs his eyes. "What indeed? Like many of—ah—his associates, Mr. Fang took pains to guard his memoir against casual inspection. The book is encrypted."

"Encrypted!"

"It is simple enough, but to work in cipher *and* Chinese at the same time … ah." Mo puts his glasses back into place on his nose. He regards Penumbra quietly. Then, he speaks: "This is not an ordinary bookstore."

"Indeed. It seems more akin to a youth hostel—"

"No, no, not that," Mo says, shaking his head; his glasses glint like searchlights. "They will go as quickly as they came

… they are already going. Haven't you heard, Mr. Penumbra? Their Summer of Love is fading."

"No, I had not heard. But then—well. I did not come to San Francisco for the Summer of Love."

"Of course, of course. Drugs, music, a new age dawning … and you came for an old book."

Penumbra recoils, stung. But he sees that Mo is smiling: not with any kind of mockery, but with genuine warmth.

"Mr. Corvina also came to this city looking for a book," Mo says. "He came from—where was it? San Diego, I believe. I do not think he intended to stay, but I offered him a post as my clerk, and, well. There he sits."

"You have both been very helpful."

"Yes, well. Mr. Corvina is quite engaged by your quest, you know. He told me we ought to help you however we can. I told him it was foolishness."

Stung again. "I am sorry that you feel that way, Mr. Al-Asmari."

This time, Mo suffers the honorific without complaint. "I have known people like you before, Mr. Penumbra. People with your gift."

"Oh, if I have any skill at research, it is only—"

"No, no. Anyone can fuss in the archives. I am speaking of the willingness to entertain absurd ideas. It is a habit that is highly prized among … my peers."

Penumbra is silent at that.

"I wish that I possessed it myself, but alas, I can only appreciate it." Mo sips his coffee. "Well. I suppose I can do more than that. I can follow Mr. Corvina's exhortation and find a way to assist you. Tell me about this map."

Penumbra shows Mo what he's discovered. Under the lamplight, he points to number 43, the *William Gray*, and to the BART tunnel's intercept course.

Mo frowns. "Here, I must demonstrate my failing, Mr. Penumbra, and tell you the truth: it's extremely unlikely that anything remains down there."

"You are right," Penumbra says, "and yet, the letter from San Francisco mentioned a 'place of safekeeping.' It is possible—not probable, I admit—but *possible* that the *Tycheon* was somehow protected."

"There! Your gift. I would like nothing more than for you to be correct, and perhaps for other treasures to be preserved there, as well … you see? It is mildly contagious." He laces his fingers together and rests his chin there. "What do you need from me, Mr. Penumbra?"

"Well. I do not—ah. I know the ship's location, and I know that the excavation suggests … the possibility of access. But, in truth—" He lets out a single great guffaw, laughing at his own foolishness. "—I have no idea what to do with this information!"

Mo's face splits into a grin. "Oh, I know what to do, Mr. Penumbra. More coffee? Good—yes, I know exactly what to do."

MEMBERS ONLY

MOHAMMED AL-ASMARI HAS a posse—or at least that's how he makes it sound, conferring with Penumbra and Corvina down on the floor of the bookstore, across the bulk of the wide desk.

"The measure of a bookstore is not its receipts, but its friends," he says, "and here, we are rich indeed." Penumbra sees Corvina clench his jaw just slightly; he gets the sense that Mo's clerk wishes they had some receipts, too.

"They reside in every part of this city," Mo continues. "Every neighborhood, every social stratum. I assure you, someone will know someone … who knows someone … who is connected to this excavation." He divvies up the labor: "I will make the calls. Mr. Corvina, you will do the legwork. But while you are occupied … someone must take your place here." He swivels to look at Penumbra.

"Me?"

"Are we to be collaborators in this quest or not?"

"Well. I suppose—yes. I can watch the store."

Corvina eyes Mo darkly. "Are you going to tell him the rules?"

"Of course." Mo draws himself up straight. "Mr. Penumbra: Please make yourself at home here. Do whatever you must to prevent the store from being ransacked, burned down, or raided by the police. Sell a few books if you can. But do not, under any circumstances, browse, read, or otherwise inspect the shelved volumes."

Penumbra peers up at the tall shelves. "They are off-limits entirely?"

"If you are called upon by a member to retrieve one, you may do so."

"A member. I see. How does one *become* a member?"

Mo adjusts his glasses. "There is a way of progressing through this bookstore. Before one can become a member, one must be a customer. And—ah, wait." He plays at recollecting: "Have you by chance … purchased a book yet, Mr. Penumbra?"

He smiles, shakes his head. "I have not."

Mo smiles, too. "Then spend some time browsing, why don't you? I recommend the poetry table. Have you read Brautigan? Oh, you must, you must."

Penumbra takes Corvina's place that night and presides over the clamor of the 24-Hour Bookstore. He fears the long-haired throng will consider him even more hopelessly square than Corvina, but in fact, they seem to regard him as a novelty, and one by one, they wander over to chat. The customer named Coyote asks for help finding *Rosemary's Baby* and then actually buys it. The woman with the portable radio inquires about Corvina, then reveals that the bushy-bearded duo orbiting the CINEMA table, George and Francis, are local filmmakers. Felix presents his now preposterously tattered copy of *Dune* and asks if he can trade it in for *The Drowned World*. Penumbra is not sure if that is part of Mo's business model, but he says yes anyway.

Later, with the scrum at its swollen peak, a dark-eyed woman glances at Penumbra: once, twice. Then she crosses the store, a plume of smoke tracking her progress, like a little steam engine. When she draws near, Penumbra can see that she is carrying a slender joint. She holds it out toward him.

"Want some, tiger?"

"Ah—no. In fact, I do not think ... you see, there are books here."

"Oh, I'm no book-burner."

"It would presumably be an accident."

"No such thing as accidents, tiger." She takes a drag. "You're new here, aren't you?"

"New? Ah, no. In point of fact, I am not truly here." He means to say: I do not work here; I am just filling in. But it comes out strangely, and—

"That's far out," she says, nodding. "Maybe I'm not here either. Maybe you and me shouldn't be here—together. Catch my drift?"

"I believe so, but I do not—"

"My pals are heading over to the Haight. Why don't you boogie with us?"

"I cannot, ah, boogie. That is—I cannot leave my post. Another time, perhaps."

She gives him a pitying smile. "Keep on trucking, then." She sends another plume curling into the air and rejoins the crowd. Later, heading for the door, she casts one last glance in his direction, but Penumbra looks away.

Bright clear sunlight presses in through the front windows and gleams on bare floorboards; Al-Asmari's 24-Hour Bookstore is, remarkably, empty. It is midday, and the longhairs are probably in the park, sprawled on the grass under the strange light of the daystar. The store is stuffy and overheated, unequipped for this level of thermodynamic stress; Penumbra has propped the door open with a stack of *Slaughterhouse-Five*s.

He is watching the shop again, waiting for Corvina's return. The clerk has found a member with a brother-in-law who does taxes for a construction company that manages one of the BART worksites. He is schmoozing the accountant over beers at the House of Shields.

Penumbra is halfway through *The Electric Kool-Aid Acid Test*; he feels like he understands the overnight crowd better with every page. The Merry Pranksters have just encountered a group of Hells Angels when a throat is cleared, delicately.

Penumbra snaps his head up, startled. Before him, several steps back from the desk, stands a young woman in a green corduroys.

"Can I—ah." Penumbra sets his book aside. "Can I help you?"

The woman seems to be evaluating him. Penumbra is not sure how long she has been standing there. She is clutching a huge dark-bound book close to her chest.

"You're new," she says at last.

"I am not actually—ah." He gives in. "Yes. I suppose I am new."

"I can come back later."

"No, no. I can help you."

She takes two swift steps forward, drops the book onto the desk with a heavy *whump*, then retreats two steps back. "I'm done with that one."

Penumbra tips the book up, looks at the spine. It is one of the volumes from the tall shelves.

"Of course," he says. "So. How, er—was it?"

She is silent a moment, and he thinks she might be about to flee out the front door, but then her cool countenance cracks a little, as if she can't quite contain herself, and in a rush, she says: "It was pretty interesting. Not as hard as I thought it would be, from the way he talked about it. Mo, I mean. It was just a homophonic substitution cipher." She pauses. "Maybe I shouldn't have told you that."

Penumbra has no idea what she is talking about. Or what

he is supposed to do now. An uncomfortable silence spreads between them.

"Anyway," she says at last. "The next one in the sequence is … wait." She digs in her pocket, pulls out a wrinkled piece of paper. It is covered on both sides with letters scratched out and rewritten, blanks erased and filled in, like a game of Hangman gone wrong. She reads across and down, mouthing the letters. Then she refolds the paper, stuffs it back into her pocket, and announces: "Kingslake."

"Kingslake," Penumbra repeats. He finds the oblong ledger that Corvina consulted on his first visit—the catalog. The entries are handwritten; many are annotated, and some are crossed out. He finds KAEL, KANE (SEE ALSO: CAIN), ~~KEANE~~, KIM, KING, and then, KINGSLAKE. The catalog specifies coordinates.

"Three … twenty-three," Penumbra reads. "Three twenty-three. Wait here, please."

He pads back toward the tall shelves, where he finds numbered brass plaques set low, at approximately Al-Asmari-level. He follows them down to III and rolls the ladder into place, fumbling with the locking brace at the bottom.

Then he climbs. It turns out that shelf XXIII is very far from the ground. The Galvanic library has no ladders; there, they keep the books, sensibly, on many separate floors. Penumbra grips the rungs tightly and takes slow, careful steps—past V, past X, past XV and XX.

At this height, he can see the ceiling—can confirm that there is, in fact, a ceiling, not just an infinity of dark shelving.

He tips his head back to get a better look. There is an image up there, a mural that covers the whole area, looking a bit like a Renaissance fresco. Piece by piece, he assembles the scene: climbers in cloaks on a steep rocky trail. Dark clouds above them, and lightning that runs like a crack through the paint. Their expressions show wide eyes and gritted teeth, but their arms are outstretched, and they clasp hands. The climbers are pulling each other along.

He lowers his gaze to find shelf XXIII and there he spies his quarry: it is as thick as a dictionary, with KINGSLAKE printed on the spine. He hooks an elbow around the ladder, then unclamps his other hand and sends it searching after the book, his longest finger stretching to reach it, wiggling in air, just catching the spine once, twice, tipping it forward, until it starts to slide under its own weight, and he knows he needs to grab it, except that he is suddenly very aware of its mass, and he is afraid that if he attaches himself to this heavy object, it might overburden him, might pull him—

The book falls.

He has time to register his carelessness, and even consider how else he might have approached this challenge, as he watches it plunge down past twenty-two lower shelves, spinning end over end, fluttering just slightly—and fall into the outstretched arms of Marcus Corvina.

Down on the floor, the young woman has a look of horror—perhaps potential co-culpability?—rising in her eyes. She accepts the book from Corvina, whispers a quiet thank-you, and darts for the door. The clerk opens the wide leather-bound book on the desk and begins to scribble there.

Penumbra approaches gingerly. "I am sorry, Marcus," he ventures. "I should not have—"

Corvina looks up. He is smiling—only the second time Penumbra has seen that expression on his face. "I've dropped three books and never breathed a word to Mo. As far as I'm concerned … I didn't see a thing."

Penumbra nods. "Thank you."

Corvina finishes scribbling, closes the leather-bound book, then taps it meaningfully. "It's people like Evelyn Erdos who are the real customers, you know."

"The real customers."

"Yes. The real *readers*." The smile has faded. "If I ran this store, I'd make it members only. I certainly wouldn't waste any more time with the public." He almost spits it: *public*.

Penumbra pauses, considering. Then he says: "Marcus … if this store were not open to the public, I would not be here now."

Corvina furrows his brow and nods once. But he seems unswayed.

The clerk's schmoozing has been fruitful. The member's brother-in-law's client, Frank Lapin, manages one of the BART worksites, and he is amenable to their undertaking; in other words, he will happily accept a bribe to look the other way while they explore the excavation.

Corvina delivers the news glumly.

"But this is a positive development, isn't it?" Penumbra asks.

"He wants two thousand dollars," Corvina explains. "I wish I could tell you otherwise, but we don't have that kind of money." He looks around the store with a sour expression. "As you might have noticed, we don't sell many books here. A foundation in New York pays the rent … but that's about it."

"Do not despair yet, Marcus," Penumbra says. "There is another benefactor we can call upon."

Penumbra dials Langston Armitage from a pay phone on Montgomery Street. He explains what he has learned. He describes the city, the ship, the map. He tells him about the bookstore.

Armitage is wary. "Who is this bookseller?" he croaks. "Some purveyor of pulp?"

"No, no," Penumbra says. "Mohammed Al-Asmari is anything but that. I have visited every bookstore in this city, and many beyond, and this one … this man … they are unique."

"But he's still just a bookseller, my boy. Commercial. Not academic. Not intellectual. All he cares about, at the end of the day, is selling books."

Penumbra barks a laugh. "I am not so sure about that."

"What keeps the lights on, then?" Armitage challenges. "It's a business, my boy."

"I would say this establishment occupies a … gray area, sir."

"Playing in the shadows, are we, Penumbra? Ah. There is a precedent. Did I ever tell you about the time Beacham got himself hired by the publisher in Hungary, just to get at their secret archives?"

"No, sir."

"Well. We found him floating facedown in the Danube, but no matter."

Penumbra explains to his employer that, if they want access to the remains of the *William Gray*, it will come at considerable cost.

"And to be very clear, sir," he says, "the ship is likely little more than a compressed layer of rotten wood at this point. I still think it is worth trying, but … there is no guarantee that the *Tycheon* has been preserved in any form."

"Well, you know our saying: 'It's not over until you hold the book's ashes in your hands, weeping at the years you've lost.'"

"I did not know we had that saying, sir."

"I'll wire you the money, my boy. Bring us a book!"

THE SANDHOG COMETH

PENUMBRA ARRIVES EARLY, in time to watch the last remnants of the overnight crowd rouse themselves, stretch languidly, and drift out in search of various sustenances. By midday, the store has emptied, and Corvina has put him to work, rearranging a short span of books midway up the tall shelves. They climb two ladders side by side and hand heavy volumes back and forth according to some system that Penumbra does not understand.

As they work, they talk. Penumbra tells the clerk about Galvanic, and the library there. He learns that Corvina was, in fact, a sailor of sorts: a radar technician aboard an aircraft carrier. He spent four years at sea.

"I read a lot," Corvina says. "That's how I got interested in all of this."

"What sort of things did you read?"

"What *didn't* I read? I read everything. We had the best library in the whole navy. The officer who oversaw it—I only learned this later—he's part of the same … organization as Mo. He taught me to read Greek."

"Wait. You are saying that your *aircraft carrier* was related to this store somehow?"

"Absolutely. Midshipman Taylor's Fourth-Deck Book Depository. There's a whole network of these places … it's a tradition, Ajax. It goes back a long way."

"So, that makes two floating bookstores, then."

Corvina laughs. "Ha. Yes. The *William Gray* and the *Coral Sea*. Although, I have to tell you … mine was bigger." He smiles. Number three.

After an hour, Penumbra's back aches; his calves tremble; his hands feel like claws. He is about to beg for a break when the bell tinkles below, and a rough voice calls out: "Anybody home?" Louder: "Anybody named Mark here?"

Corvina's face goes sharp. He hisses: "It's him!" Penumbra begins to descend, but Corvina hisses again. "No. I told his accountant I would be alone. You stay here."

Before Penumbra can protest, Corvina curls his ankles around the sides of the ladder, let his hands go slack, and—Penumbra gasps—slides straight down, falling into a liquid crouch on the floor. He rises smoothly and strides through the shelves toward the front of the store, passing out of Penumbra's view, into the sunlight.

"Welcome," Penumbra hears Corvina say.

"Heya, Mark." The visitor's voice is rough and jocular.

"Marcus," Corvina corrects him. "You're Alvin's client? The construction worker?"

"Construction worker? Please! I'm a sandhog. The few, the proud. Good to meet you. I'm Frankie. Or maybe you prefer Franklin."

If there is a note of mockery there, Corvina either does not detect it or chooses to ignore it. "Franklin. It's good to meet you, too. Alvin told you about the nature of my undertaking?"

Penumbra slows his breathing, stretches his ears to listen. Frankie must be wearing work boots; whenever he moves, they clomp heavily on the floorboards.

"He did, and—I gotta ask this, I'm sorry. For my own peace of mind. You're not a bank robber, are you?"

"I assure you," Corvina replies smoothly, "I am merely a local historian."

"Okay. I'm gonna trust you. But only because Alvin's a good guy, and because he vouches for you. Got that?"

"Of course. Now … how should we proceed?"

"Well, first of all, Mark—you pay me. The amount you, ah, suggested to Alvin will be just fine."

Penumbra hears the scrape of a drawer, the whisper of paper—the fat envelope he retrieved from Wells Fargo yesterday. He feels a thrill down his spine. This is what it means to be a Junior Acquisitions Officer.

"Here," Corvina says. "Just as we discussed."

"Let me just give that a look-see." There's a rip, a riffle.

The counting of cash. “Very generous. Okay, Mark, I got good news and I got bad news.”

“I’m not sure I like the sound of that.”

“The good news is, your spot’s all clear. We dug through there ages ago. Market and Beale, right? Yeah, I went back and checked it out myself. There’s something there. Doesn’t look too great, but considering the circumstances, it doesn’t look too terrible either.”

“And the bad news?”

“The bad news, Mark ... is I don’t manage the Embarcadero worksite. That’s a whole different outfit, and it’s locked up tight.”

Penumbra can almost hear Corvina’s nostrils flare. His own heart sinks. They are so close, and yet, once again, the path is blocked. This is what it means to be a Junior Acquisitions Officer.

Corvina presses ahead. “You wouldn’t be here if you didn’t have a solution,” he says. “Am I right?”

“You’re very perceptive, Mark. I’ve got you covered. We finished the tube—did you know that?”

“The tube under the bay?”

The visitor makes a satisfied *mm-hmm*. “Sealed it up tight. No track yet, but we’re driving trucks through every day. And the worksite on the *other* side of the tube—that one’s mine. I can square things away with the night watchman, no problem.”

“The worksite ... on the other side.”

“Yeah. West Oakland.”

Corvina chuckles. "You're suggesting we go the long way."

Frankie laughs, too. "Why not? Get a little exercise, right?"

"Is it safe?"

"Sure. The muckety-mucks are organizing a big walk next month—open to the public. Little kids, old folks, everybody. Right through the tube. The way I see it, you're just getting early access."

"Well, I'm glad you see it that way. I assume that this donation ensures your ... discretion."

"Of course, Mark, of course." Frankie clomps toward the door, then pauses. Penumbra hears him turn. "What's in there, anyway? Gold doubloons?"

"Would you care?"

"I don't know .... I might want a cut."

"I hate to disappoint you, Franklin, but it's just books."

"Well, this seems like a lot to pay for some old books, but I can see you have, ah, quite a collection here. To each his own, I always say. You all set?"

"West Oakland. Through the tube. What do I say to the night watchman?"

"His name's Hector. He'll keep an eye out for you. We can use a password—"

"Festina lente."

"Say again now?"

"*Festina lente*. That will be our password." It is possible, Penumbra realizes, that this is not Corvina's first time organizing an illicit expedition.

"Fes-teen-uh lenty. Okay. If you say so." Frankie clomps toward the door again, and this time he pulls it open. The bell tinkles brightly. "Go anytime after midnight. Fes-teen-uh lenty. Okay. Good luck down there, Mark."

THE WRECK OF THE *WILLIAM GRAY*

THEY CROSS THE bay on the last ferry of the night under a half moon flickering spookily through low clouds. The boat passes smoothly beneath the dark bulk of the Bay Bridge, sterner and more serious-looking than its tourist-friendly cousin.

The ferry lands near the Port of Oakland, among the warehouses. They have bicycles, purchased from a man who called himself Russian Mike on the corner of Turk and Leavenworth. Corvina claims the sleek green Schwinn; Penumbra gets the blue beach cruiser with a banana seat. They pedal to the West Oakland worksite, which is not difficult to identify: there are smooth concrete pillars rising to support nothing; hills of rust-red rebar waiting to be woven into stone; multiple slumbering backhoes.

They spot Hector shuffling lazily around the chain-link perimeter, wearing an approximation of a police uniform. They signal from a distance; approach cautiously; say *festina lente* in the shadows. He grunts, waves them through, and continues around the fence, all without ever quite looking them in the face.

The mouth of the Transbay Tube gapes hugely. Loose dirt hangs ragged around its metal lip; it looks less like a public works project and more like an ancient tomb. There is no train track yet. Instead, a wide, weedy path descends from the worksite, marked with treads where trucks have passed.

There are no lights. They are prepared for this. Corvina lifts a camping lantern and hangs it from his handlebars. "Ready?"

Penumbra steadies himself. "I suppose so."

The tube swallows them. Corvina zips out ahead, pedaling with long sure strokes, his gearshift clucking and crackling as he moves swiftly to the most efficient ratio. Penumbra glances back, watching the view through the tube's entrance—a dusty oval of Oakland sky—shrink and fade until it is no brighter than the blotches of color that his retinas produce in the absence of light.

It is darkness of a kind and quality that he has never experienced. The floor of the tube is smooth under his tires; it feels like he is racing indoors, across a basketball court or a bank lobby. There is, every few seconds, a dull *whump* as he crosses one of the tube's seams: the places where the huge metal segments have been joined together and sealed against the bay.

The bay is out there. Up there. How deep is it? Penumbra has no idea. It might be ten feet; it might be a hundred. The air has changed. It is cold and damp, thick with the smell of trapped exhaust. He wonders if there is enough oxygen down here, really? What if the work crews have not yet prepared it for human traffic? What if he and Corvina swoon halfway through? What if no one finds them until morning?

Corvina is racing ahead. The lantern's spark bobs and dips on his handlebars and casts a crazy shadow behind him, a dark avatar that dances and leaps across the floor of the tube.

Penumbra cries out: "Slow down!"—but Corvina doesn't hear him, or he can't understand, or he won't listen. Penumbra sucks in a lungful of heavy air and cries again: "*Could you please*—ah." He gives up. Corvina's shadow recedes; the spark grows smaller. The darkness clamps down.

Penumbra comes to a halt, his chest heaving. He rests on the handlebars, which he can feel but not see. Corvina's lantern shrinks to nothing.

He is a man unaccustomed to anger but he feels it now. Corvina! He is, Penumbra realizes, not the man to follow into a terrifying subterranean tunnel. He is capable, yes, and commanding—but he has no patience for anyone who cannot keep up.

Well.

He cannot stand here forever.

Penumbra pedals slowly forward, testing. It is all darkness ahead, a pure blank void—but, of course, there are no obstacles. Nothing stands in his way. He feels the bicycle's front wheel rise, realizes he is climbing the curve of the tube; he jerks the handlebars, allows gravity pull him back down. This can work. He simply has to go by feel, let the curves do their work. He simply has to keep pedaling. He can close his eyes. There is nothing that can hurt him here.

He loses track of time. The whole universe contracts into the almost philosophical darkness of the tube, the curve of its space-time that he tracks with his legs, not with his eyes. Perhaps he will emerge and find that ten years have passed. Fifty. He smiles at that, and does the math, counting the years in time with the pedals: 2017 … 2018 … 2019. How will this city look in the twenty-first century? Maybe those Yerba Buena Gardens will finally have a plant or—

Corvina cries out. "Ajax! Is that you?"

Penumbra comes to a skidding stop. "Where are you?"

"Here, here." His voice cries bleakly out of the darkness nearby; Penumbra can almost see him, a dark outline against the deeper darkness of the tube. Corvina appears to be sitting on the ground. "I need help, I need … it's too dark, Ajax. I lost the lantern."

Penumbra lays his bicycle gently on the floor of the tube and shuffles toward the sound of Corvina's voice. "I am coming," he says. "Hold out your hands."

His fingers brush something in the darkness, and a hand clamps tight around his wrist—strong, shaking, slippery with sweat.

"You are fine, Marcus." He hoists him up, or tries

to; Corvina nearly tips him over. The sheer mass of him! Penumbra grunts and heaves, and the clerk rises. "You are just fine."

They walk together for a long time, Penumbra leading Corvina by the hand. The clerk says nothing, just follows, his breath slowing down, evening out. His fingers are thick and meaty but very soft.

Finally: *fiat lux*. There is a fuzzy suggestion of light that becomes a pinprick, then a dot. The faster they walk, the faster it grows, so they walk very fast indeed, until they are running, and somewhere in the process Corvina drops Penumbra's hand and charges ahead.

At the end, the tube rises again, and when they emerge into the light of the Embarcadero worksite, Corvina is himself again. He betrays no sign of his ordeal in the darkness.

"The ship will be nearby," he says crisply. Taking command again.

The tube opens into a cavernous space lit with bulbs in cages, a festive string of them hanging from the rough-hewn ceiling. The space is supported by a frame of dark girders, and in places, a concrete perimeter is rising. Water pools on the ground in puddles too wide to leap across, so they walk straight through. It fills Penumbra's shoes.

There are signs of life and work: cast-off gloves, paper cups, a rogue safety helmet. The helmet is white plastic, with the BART logo printed in blue across the brow. Penumbra picks it up, gives it a shake, sets it on his head. “What do you think?”

Corvina snorts. “You’re the skinniest sandhog in the city.”

More than a hundred years ago, the *William Gray* was scuttled and buried under a pile of rubble. Drowned and crushed. The mast snapped long ago; the sails and rigging decomposed. All that remained was the ship’s hull, and that only barely, like a soda can crumpled in a trash heap.

Then the BART crew came tunneling through the heap. Penumbra has seen fossils preserved in stone, great slabs split apart to show an ancient beast in cross section; this is precisely how the *William Gray* looks now. Its shape is dark but distinct in the wall of the tunnel. Here in the city’s second subbasement, a shadow of the ship still remains.

It is, once again, a moment of triumph that fades quickly into defeat. Penumbra had imagined something like a shipwreck, the kind he has seen in a Jacques Cousteau film. He had imagined some sort of space they could penetrate and explore, but that seems foolish now. Their quarry is not archaeological but geological. It is a fossil, through and through.

“Here,” Corvina calls. Penumbra snaps out of his gloomy reverie. The clerk has found two shovels elsewhere in the worksite. He tosses one lightly to Penumbra, who slips and drops it.

"Marcus, it is not—"

"I see a ship," Corvina declares. "I see this city's first bookstore. Surely, Ajax, there is something to discover here."

"You share my gift, Marcus," Penumbra says dryly.

"What gift?"

"Mr. Al-Asmari called it that. 'The willingness to entertain absurd ideas.' "

Corvina snorts. "I don't *entertain* ideas," he says. "I work for them." He slides his shovel's blade into the tunnel's wall and begins to dig.

An hour passes. Maybe more. They dig deeper into the remains of the ship, throwing shovelfuls of dirt and silt and decomposed wood over their heads, making a dank pile behind them. Penumbra's shovel slices through clots of soft matter that are, he suspects, the sad remains of books. They are dark and sodden, rotted and ruined, but he can see the suggestions of spines.

Black muck spatters and soaks his shirt and pants. The deeper they go, the worse the smell—a century of rot, finally released. Penumbra's arms are burning, his feet are soaked, and he can tell that even Corvina is tiring, when—

TONK.

His shovel hits something that is not soft and ruined. He pulls it back, swings again.

TONK.

"Marcus, I think perhaps …" he begins to say, but the

clerk is already there, swinging with his own shovel. They trace the edge of the hard, *TONK*ing shape, then excavate around it, until Corvina is able to use his shovel as a lever. He gives a sharp grunt; a small metal trunk pops out of the hole, lands on the bottom of the tunnel with a wet *thud*, balances on its end, and falls over.

Penumbra and Corvina stare at each other, wide-eyed.

The trunk is heavily corroded, its surface boiling with rusty warts and green-brown streaks, but it seems to be intact. There is a supremely fat padlock holding the lid tight.

"Stand back," Corvina says. He lifts his shovel high and brings it down like a wrathful bolt. The fat old padlock does not so much break as crumble, with what seems, to Penumbra, something like relief.

Later, they hike up through the worksite, Corvina carrying the chest. The Embarcadero night watchman spots them from the other side of the giant hole in the ground. He shouts: "You! Hey! What are you doing there?"

"Don't stop," Corvina whispers. There is a line of orange cones just ahead, and beyond them, the sidewalk, where couples in coats and scarves hustle past, none sparing a glance for the gulch to their side. Behind them, the dark wall of the Embarcadero freeway blots out the sky, and on both of its decks, cars whiz through the night, honking and squealing. The light and noise is like a balm after the tunnel below.

Penumbra turns toward the watchman and taps his

helmet. “Just finishing some work! You know how it is. *Festina lente!*” With that, they are past the cones, onto the sidewalk, and free.

The craft of fortune is theirs.

A MILLION RANDOM DIGITS

THIS TIME, MO really does chase them out. The long-hairs mutter and moan, but he insists: "There is a lovely bookstore just up the street. The lights might be doused, but don't let that fool you … keep knocking. Ask for Lawrence."

Penumbra clears the wide desk, and Corvina deposits their haul, the contents of the chest: seven volumes, each dry and intact, each wrapped in a swaddling of calfskin. Mo is agog. They are all agog. One by one, they unwrap the treasures.

"Madrigal!" Mo exclaims. Then, even louder: "Brito! He was one of the first generation!"

One of the books is bound in leather, twin to the book on the desk, but where that one has a Roman numeral five on the spine, this volume is numbered one. Mo turns it over in his hands. "The first logbook," he breathes. "This is the record of our earliest customers. It's rumored that Mark Twain was among them. Now we'll know for sure."

Corvina unwraps one of the last remaining volumes, and wordlessly, he passes it to Penumbra. It is dull gray, discolored in spots, like a caterpillar evicted from its chrysalis. The cover, in unadorned caps, says TECHNE TYCHEON. Penumbra opens the book to show its first page.

It is a jumble of phrases lined up in rows and columns. Each one seems to be just a fragment: THE GREAT RIVER, BRANCHING AND MERGING; ROAR OF A TYRANT LION; THERE ARE NO WALLS WITHOUT BRICKS; YOUR DEAD GRANDFATHER'S LAUGHING SKULL ...

He flips to the next page—more of the same. THE PRINCE WAS A LIZARD ALL ALONG. Picks a random page in the middle of the book—even more. YOUR TEETH FALLING OUT, ONE BY ONE. Each page is a rough grid, and each space in the grid contains some fragment, some image.

It is incomprehensible.

This book of prophecy, Penumbra realizes, is elaborately encrypted. His heart sinks. He has seen volumes like this before; Occult Lit 337 was devoted to *Codes and Ciphers*. Now, looking at the *Tycheon*, he sees homework. He sees years of painstaking labor.

Mo smiles encouragingly. "If there is a code, it can be cracked, Mr. Penumbra. Perhaps I can interest Mr. Fedorov in the task ...."

Penumbra's head snaps up. "Wait—what do you mean?"

"He is our most skilled code-breaker," Mo explains. "He has made quick work of previous volumes, and with luck—"

"But I intend to take this book back to Galvanic." Penumbra's words hang in the air. Corvina extends a hand, settles it firmly on the *Tycheon*'s cover.

"Mr. Penumbra, this book belongs to us," Mo says. "It belonged to us on the day the *William Gray* sank. This small matter of a century-long entombment does not change that fact."

Penumbra shakes his head. "You are welcome to the others, but I was able to fund this undertaking only because of my employer's interest in this book. It belongs in our library, where scholars will make sense of it. It cannot stay here. This—" He gestures in a wide circle. "—this is just a bookstore."

Mo's face flashes at that, but before he can reply, and to Penumbra's surprise, Corvina interjects. "Mo. Ajax is right. He paid for this. If we'd been able to fund it ourselves—well, we couldn't." He pulls his hand back, and Penumbra snatches up the *Tycheon*.

Mo's eyes flash. "Look around, Mr. Penumbra. This is not *just* a bookstore." He turns and retreats into the tall shelves. Penumbra hears the door—the one marked MO—open and shut.

He takes the Peninsula Commute again and makes his way through Palo Alto to Claude's redwood-shadowed home. Inside, on the green carpet, where one pizza box once lay, three are now stacked. Penumbra is beginning to get a sense for the rhythm of his former roommate's life.

"I have come to say good-bye," he says, sitting cross-legged. The gray cat nuzzles his knee.

Claude frowns. "Already? Well. I'm glad you visited, buddy. What happened with that ship?"

From inside a fat manila envelope, Penumbra produces the *Tycheon*. "Our quest to find the *William Gray* was successful."

"You found it! Holy shit!"

Penumbra allows a smile. "We did, thanks in part to your guidance. And we found this book within. But now I must decide what to do with it."

"You're not taking it back to Galvanic?"

"I may, or—ah." Penumbra sighs, long and loud. "I just do not know, Claude."

"Is it valuable? What's it about, anyway? Demons?"

"It is most certainly valuable, but as to its contents … let us just say that if there are demons, they were well hidden. Look for yourself." He flips it open, shows Claude the pages of disconnected phrases. "It is encrypted. Inscrutable."

Claude's eyes flick across the fragments in quick saccades. "This is a code?"

Penumbra nods. "Very clearly so. I have seen books like this before, at Galvanic. I took a course—"

"Have you considered that it might just be random?"

"I do not think it is a book of nonsense, Claude. It would not have survived this long if there were not some sense to it—some value."

"Oh! You think something has to have *sense* to have *value*? Buddy ... did I ever show you the RAND book?"

"You did not."

Claude hops up and walks to one of the far piles. He digs deep, casting thick volumes aside, throwing them across the carpet. Penumbra sees an *SDS-940 Technical Operating Manual.* He sees a slim pamphlet titled *RFC 1: Host Software.*

"Here!" Claude unearths a fat book with a dark cover and plops it down on the carpet between them. The title is set in a calm serif.

A Million Random Digits
with 100,000 Normal Deviates

"This used to be the most valuable book in this room," Claude declares. "RAND—the think tank, you know?—they published it in, let's see—" He heaves the book open, finds its copyright page. "—1946. New computers can generate their own random numbers ... well, pseudo-random, technically ... but back at Galvanic, when I needed random numbers, I copied them out of this." He flops the book open to an interior page, which is nothing but numbers in a grid, like bricks in a wall. He flips to another page. It is just the same—and also, apparently, completely different.

Penumbra traces a finger down the page. "But why? What requires this much randomness?"

"The Monte Carlo method," Claude explains. "One of the linchpins of modern science. It's the cosmic casino, buddy.

How to explain it … let's see. Sometimes, you're stuck with a system too complicated to model completely. I mean, this guy—" He pats his home-brew computer on the side. "—is powerful, but not *that* powerful. So, instead of calculating the whole system, top to bottom, you pick some random points … you place some bets. And it's just like a casino: if you place *enough* bets, the randomness evens out. You see the shape of the system underneath."

"For what might this method be used?"

"Everything!" Claude exclaims. "Climate models … economic projections … nuclear physics." He pauses, and his face goes hard. "Buddy. They used this book to make the bomb."

Penumbra chews on that. "And you believe the *Tycheon* might have similar applications."

"I don't know. If you think of the brain as a kind of system—no way can you model the whole thing. So maybe your book provides the random points. Instead of point *X*, *Y*, *Z* inside a uranium core, it's—" He glances down at the book, reads one of the fragments there. "—'the Crown of the False King' inside a human brain." He pauses. "Ha. That makes me think of my boss. See? Randomness can be productive." Claude pauses, struck by a thought. Suddenly, his eyes are merry. "I never told you this, but I found the matching algorithm."

Penumbra frowns, confused. "Which—?"

"The algorithm that matched us at Galvanic—the great *computerized process*, remember? I was digging around in the basement, and I found the cards with the source code. You want to know how it worked?"

"How?"

"It was random."

"Random," Penumbra repeats.

"Completely random."

"The computer did not know we both had so many books?"

Claude shakes his head. "I think the math department got lazy. I'm pretty sure the president never had a clue. I mean, it was *completely* random."

Penumbra laughs at that—a single great, barking guffaw. Claude smiles, and then he laughs, too, and soon they are laughing together on the green shag carpet, with the fuzzy gray cat yowling along.

CLIMBERS

HE STANDS BEFORE Langston Armitage on the top floor of the library and delivers the *Techne Tycheon*. The old frog unwraps his treasure slowly, eyes wide and devouring. Penumbra narrates the book's recovery. He explains its probable use, as a kind of random prompt for fortune-telling, like tarot cards or the *I Ching*.

"Well done, my boy, well done," Armitage croaks, effusive. "Books of randomness … this might necessitate a new course offering. The number would have to be random, of course … different each year. Say, English 389. Is that random? No, I don't think so. In any case." He sets the book to one side. "Did you hear that Lemire died? It was his old wound, the one that never healed. From the Mongolian expedition. It finally killed him. My point is, his post is open. He was a Senior Acquisitions Officer, my boy."

Bright sunlight presses in through the strip of green

wallpaper. Outside, Penumbra knows, it is nothing but cornfields for miles and miles.

"I am grateful for the offer, sir," he says, "but I have decided to return to San Francisco."

Armitage's lips pull into a tight line. "San Francisco," he repeats. This time, he does not break into song.

The bell above the door tinkles. Penumbra finds Corvina and Mo huddled across the wide desk, deep in deliberation. They turn, and the surprise is plain on their faces. He says nothing; instead, he makes his way slowly through the tables, wandering and browsing. Corvina and Mo are silent as they watch him meander from POETRY to PSYCHEDELIA to MO'S PICKS. When he reaches them, he takes a breath and announces: "I have delivered the *Tycheon* to my former employer at Galvanic."

Corvina nods slowly. Mo does, too, and says: "It was your right, Mr. Penumbra. I should never have suggested otherwise. Well. I can only say that it was a rare pleasure to—"

"I would like to purchase this," Penumbra interrupts, sliding a book across the desk. It is a new paperback edition of *Through the Looking-Glass* with a mildly hallucinogenic cover. Corvina raises an eyebrow. Mo cocks his head; waiting.

Penumbra continues: "And I would like to inquire about … membership."

Mo's face splits into a grin. "Of course, of course. Ring

him up, Mr. Corvina!" He pauses. "Did I hear you correctly? Did you say your *former* employer, Mr. Penumbra?"

"I did, Mr. Al-Asmari. I have relocated. I am staying with a friend in Palo Alto until I find a place of my own. In the city."

Mo circles around to join Penumbra at the front of the desk. "Then perhaps we should entertain … a rather absurd idea. Perhaps we should entertain the idea of *employment*." Mo peers up at the younger man, his round glasses glinting. "Tell me, how do you feel about those ladders?"

Thanksgiving. It's cold again, but the morning is bright and clear. Penumbra is alone in the bookstore; Corvina is away in New York, on what Mo dubs a research trip.

The bell above the door tinkles. Penumbra looks up from his labors at the logbook to see Claude Novak stepping into the store.

"Nice digs, buddy."

"It is a comfortable place. At night, it becomes quite lively."

Claude wanders through the store, pausing to peruse the table marked SCIENCE FICTION. He finds a book there and brings it to the desk. *Stand on Zanzibar*.

"I'm glad you're here," Claude says. He taps the book's cover: *tap, tap tap tap*. "It's good to have you around."

"It is good to be here," Penumbra replies. "In fact, I feel almost indignant that you did not sing this city's praises more stridently. Claude, you have been hoarding California to yourself."

He laughs at that, and nods agreeably. Then he tells Penumbra that his colleagues, only days ago, established a cross-country computer link. "Not just a network," he says, "but an *inter*-network."

"What did they transmit?"

"Just a few characters—barely anything. Then it crashed. But it was pretty neat. It was—huh." He stops in midthought, really noticing, for the first time, the tall shelves rising in the back of the store. "What *are* those?"

Claude takes a step forward, magnetized, inter-networks forgotten. He stares up into the shadows, the books in rows and columns extending into what looks like infinity. He cannot see the ceiling; cannot see the dark mural commissioned by Mr. Fang himself. It is visible only to those who climb the ladders to the very top, and if Ajax Penumbra, in later years, climbs them less, he never forgets for a moment what is painted there.

Climbers in cloaks on a steep rocky trail, arms outstretched, clasping hands. Climbers pulling each other along.

APPENDIX

Books on display in Al-Asmari's 24-Hour Bookstore in September 1969, on the low table labeled MO'S PICKS:

The High King, Lloyd Alexander
I Know Why the Caged Bird Sings, Maya Angelou
Naked Came the Stranger, Penelope Ashe
The Edible Woman, Margaret Atwood
The Drowned World, J. G. Ballard
In Watermelon Sugar, Richard Brautigan
Stand on Zanzibar, John Brunner
The Andromeda Strain, Michael Crichton
Do Androids Dream of Electric Sheep?, Philip K. Dick
The Secret Meaning of Things, Lawrence Ferlinghetti
Fantastic Four #89, Stan Lee and Jack Kirby
The Left Hand of Darkness, Ursula K. LeGuin
The Armies of the Night, Norman Mailer
Behold the Man, Michael Moorcock

Portnoy's Complaint, Philip Roth
City of the Chasch, Jack Vance
Slaughterhouse-Five, Kurt Vonnegut
The Electric Kool-Aid Acid Test, Tom Wolfe

MR PENUMBRA RETURNS IN …

Available now in E-Book and £7.99 Paperback

Turn over for the first chapter …

HELP WANTED

LOST IN THE SHADOWS of the shelves, I almost fall off the ladder. I am exactly halfway up. The floor of the bookstore is far below me, the surface of a planet I've left behind. The tops of the shelves loom high above, and it's dark up there—the books are packed in close, and they don't let any light through. The air might be thinner, too. I think I see a bat.

I am holding on for dear life, one hand on the ladder, the other on the lip of a shelf, fingers pressed white. My eyes trace a line above my knuckles, searching the spines—and there, I spot it. The book I'm looking for.

But let me back up.

My name is Clay Jannon and those were the days when I rarely touched paper.

I'd sit at my kitchen table and start scanning help-wanted ads on my laptop, but then a browser tab would blink and

I'd get distracted and follow a link to a long magazine article about genetically modified wine grapes. Too long, actually, so I'd add it to my reading list. Then I'd follow another link to a book review. I'd add the review to my reading list, too, then download the first chapter of the book—third in a series about vampire police. Then, help-wanted ads forgotten, I'd retreat to the living room, put my laptop on my belly, and read all day. I had a lot of free time.

I was unemployed, a result of the great food-chain contraction that swept through America in the early twenty-first century, leaving bankrupt burger chains and shuttered sushi empires in its wake.

The job I lost was at the corporate headquarters of NewBagel, which was based not in New York or anywhere else with a tradition of bagel-making but instead here in San Francisco. The company was very small and very new. It was founded by a pair of ex-Googlers who wrote software to design and bake the platonic bagel: smooth crunchy skin, soft doughy interior, all in a perfect circle. It was my first job out of art school, and I started as a designer, making marketing materials to explain and promote this tasty toroid: menus, coupons, diagrams, posters for store windows, and, once, an entire booth experience for a baked-goods trade show.

There was lots to do. First, one of the ex-Googlers asked me to take a crack at redesigning the company's logo. It had been big bouncy rainbow letters inside a pale brown circle; it looked pretty MS Paint. I redesigned if using a newish typeface with sharp black serifs that I thought sort of evoked the boxes and daggers of Hebrew letters. It gave NewBagel some gravitas and it won me an award from San Francisco's AIGA chapter. Then, when I mentioned to the other ex-Googler that I knew how to code (sort of), she put me in charge of the website. So I redesigned that, too, and then managed a small marketing budget keyed to search terms like "bagel" and "breakfast" and "topology." I was also the voice of @NewBagel on Twitter and attracted a few hundred followers with a mix of breakfast trivia and digital coupons.

None of this represented the glorious next stage of human evolution, but I was learning things. I was moving up. But then the economy took a dip, and it turns out that in a recession, people want good old-fashioned bubbly oblong bagels, not smooth alien-spaceship bagels, not even if they're sprinkled with precision-milled rock salt.

The ex-Googlers were accustomed to success and they would not go quietly. They quickly rebranded to become the Old Jerusalem Bagel Company and abandoned the algorithm entirely so the bagels started coming out blackened and irregular. They instructed me to make the website look old-timey, a task that burdened my soul and earned me zero AIGA awards. The marketing budget dwindled, then disappeared. There was less and less to do. I wasn't learning anything and I wasn't moving anywhere.

Finally, the ex-Googlers threw in the towel and moved to Costa Rica. The ovens went cold and the website went dark. There was no money for severance, but I got to keep my company-issued Mac-Book and the Twitter account.

So then, after less than a year of employment, I was jobless. It turned out it was more than just the food chains that had contracted. People were living in motels and tent cities. The whole economy suddenly felt like a game of musical chairs, and I was convinced I needed to grab a seat, any seat, as fast as I could.

That was a depressing scenario when I considered the competition. I had friends who were designers like me, but they had already designed world-famous websites or advanced touch-screen interfaces, not just the logo for an upstart bagel shop. I had friends who worked at Apple. My best friend, Neel, ran his own company. Another year at NewBagel and I would have been in good shape, but I hadn't lasted long enough to build my portfolio, or even get particularly good at anything. I had an art-school thesis on Swiss typography (1957–1983) and I had a three-page website.

But I kept at it with the help-wanted ads. My standards were sliding swiftly. At first I had insisted I would only work at a company with a mission I believed in. Then I thought maybe it would be fine as long as I was learning something new. After that I decided it just couldn't be evil. Now I was carefully delineating my personal definition of evil.

It was paper that saved me. It turned out that I could stay focused on job hunting if I got myself away from the internet, so I would print out a ream of help-wanted ads, drop my phone in a drawer, and go for a walk. I'd crumple up the ads that required too much experience and deposit them in dented green trash cans along the way, and so by the time

I'd exhausted myself and hopped on a bus back home, I'd have two or three promising prospectuses folded in my back pocket, ready for follow-up.

This routine did lead me to a job, though not in the way I'd expected.

San Francisco is a good place for walks if your legs are strong. The city is a tiny square punctuated by steep hills and bounded on three sides by water, and as a result, there are surprise vistas everywhere. You'll be walking along, minding your own business with a fistful of printouts, and suddenly the ground will fall away and you'll see straight down to the bay, with the buildings lit up orange and pink along the way. San Francisco's architectural style didn't really make inroads anywhere else in the country, and even when you live here and you're used to it, it lends the vistas a strangeness: all the tall narrow houses, the windows like eyes and teeth, the wedding-cake filigree. And looming behind it all, if you're facing the right direction, you'll see the rusty ghost of the Golden Gate Bridge.

I had followed one strange vista down a line of steep stair-stepped sidewalks, then walked along the water, taking the very long way home. I had followed the line of old piers—carefully skirting the raucous chowder of Fisherman's Wharf—and watched seafood restaurants fade into nautical engineering firms and then social media startups. Finally, when my stomach rumbled, signaling its readiness for lunch, I had turned back in toward the city.

Whenever I walked the streets of San Francisco, I'd watch

for help wanted signs in windows—which is not something you really do, right? I should probably be more suspicious of those. Legitimate employers use Craigslist.

Sure enough, the 24-Hour Bookstore did not have the look of a legitimate employer:

HELP WANTED

Late Shift
Specific Requirements
Good Benefits

Now: I was pretty sure "24-Hour Bookstore" was a euphemism for something. It was on Broadway, in a euphemistic part of town. My help-wanted hike had taken me far from home; the place next door was called Booty's and it had a sign with neon legs that crossed and uncrossed.

I pushed the bookstore's glass door. It made a bell tinkle brightly up above, and I stepped slowly through. I did not realize at the time what an important threshold I had just crossed.

Inside: imagine the shape and volume of a normal bookstore turned up on its side. This place was absurdly narrow and dizzyingly tall, and the shelves went all the way up—three stories of books, maybe more. I craned my neck back (why do bookstores always make you do uncomfortable things with your neck?) and the shelves faded smoothly into the shadows in a way that suggested they might just go on forever.

The shelves were packed close together, and it felt like I was standing at the border of a forest—not a friendly California forest, either, but an old Transylvanian forest, a forest full of wolves and witches and dagger-wielding bandits all waiting just beyond moonlight's reach. There were ladders that clung to the shelves and rolled side to side. Usually those seem charming, but here, stretching up into the gloom, they were ominous. They whispered rumors of accidents in the dark.

So I stuck to the front half of the store, where bright midday light pressed in and presumably kept the wolves at bay. The wall around and above the door was glass, thick square panes set into a grid of black iron, and arched across them, in tall golden letters, it said (in reverse):

ƎЯOTƧKOOB ЯUOH-42 Ƨ'AЯBMUИƎꟼ .ЯM

Below that, set in the hollow of the arch, there was a symbol—two hands, perfectly flat, rising out of an open book.

So who was Mr. Penumbra?

"Hello, there," a quiet voice called from the stacks. A figure emerged—a man, tall and skinny like one of the ladders, draped in a light gray button-down and a blue cardigan. He tottered as he walked, running a long hand along the shelves for support. When he came out of the shadows, I saw that his sweater matched his eyes, which were also blue, riding low in nests of wrinkles. He was very old.

He nodded at me and gave a weak wave. “What do you seek in these shelves?”

That was a good line, and for some reason, it made me feel comfortable. I asked, “Am I speaking to Mr. Penumbra?”

“I am Penumbra”—he nodded—“and I am the custodian of this place.”

I didn’t quite realize I was going to say it until I did: “I’m looking for a job.”

Penumbra blinked once, then nodded and tottered over to the desk set beside the front door. It was a massive block of dark-whorled wood, a solid fortress on the forest’s edge. You could probably defend it for days in the event of a siege from the shelves.

“Employment.” Penumbra nodded again. He slid up onto the chair behind the desk and regarded me across its bulk. “Have you ever worked at a bookstore before?”

“Well,” I said, “when I was in school I waited tables at a seafood restaurant, and the owner sold his own cookbook.” It was called *The Secret Cod* and it detailed thirty-one different ways to—you get it. “That probably doesn’t count.”

“No, it does not, but no matter,” Penumbra said. “Prior experience in the book trade is of little use to you here.”

Wait—maybe this place really was all erotica. I glanced down and around, but glimpsed no bodices, ripped or otherwise. In fact, just next to me there was a stack of dusty Dashiell Hammetts on a low table. That was a good sign.

"Tell me," Penumbra said, "about a book you love."

I knew my answer immediately. No competition. I told him, "Mr. Penumbra, it's not one book, but a series. It's not the best writing and it's probably too long and the ending is terrible, but I've read it three times, and I met my best friend because we were both obsessed with it back in sixth grade." I took a breath. "I love The Dragon-Song Chronicles."

Penumbra cocked an eyebrow, then smiled. "That is good, very good," he said, and his smile grew, showing jostling white teeth.

Then he squinted at me, and his gaze went up and down. "But can you climb a ladder?"

And that is how I find myself on this ladder, up on the third floor, minus the floor, of Mr. Penumbra's 24-Hour Bookstore. The book I've been sent up to retrieve is called *Al-asmari* and it's about 150 percent of one arm-length to my left. Obviously, I need to return to the floor and scoot the ladder over. But down below, Penumbra is shouting, "Lean, my boy! Lean!"

And wow, do I ever want this job.

HELP WANTED

Good Benefits
Specific Requirements

Do you cherish the written word?
Are you open to the magic of technology?

A man once created a treasure so precious that it could only be shared by those who could appreciate its true value. To that end he disguised his creation so that it would appear worthless to uncurious eyes. Unfortunately, his precautions were too powerful, and what was once a well-kept secret is now in danger of being lost forever.

After centuries of shadows and silence, The Society of the Unbroken Spine is now seeking new members.

We seek those who are curious, discreet, observant and adventurous.

We seek those who cherish the written word and are open to the magic of technology.

We seek those who love stories in whatever form they may take.

If this sounds like you, send an electronic mail with the words **FESTINA LENTE** in the subject line to **theunbrokenspine@gmail.com** to explore what you can do for the society - and what the Society can do for you.

Festina Lente,
Mr Ajax Penumbra

QUESTIONS AND ANSWERS WITH ROBIN SLOAN

1. *Mr. Penumbra's 24-Hour Bookstore* began life as an e-book. How did it become a novel?

Several years ago, I published several short stories online, in various e-book stores and also free for the taking on my website. The response to one of the stories was palpably swifter and stronger than the rest, and that was *Mr. Penumbra's 24-Hour Bookstore*, then just 6,000 words long. I thought of the stories as prototypes of a sort, so I took that signal to heart and realized there might be more lurking in the story of a tall narrow bookstore next door to a strip club.

2. You are a debut author: what has the experience of publishing a novel been like for you?

Honestly, every step has been a surprise; I didn't know much at all about the ways that books travel through the world. In particular, though, the translations have been a surprise and a delight. When I began to write this novel,

I never imagined there might be an edition in German or Turkish or Japanese.

3. Technology is obviously having a huge impact on daily life, particularly in the world of publishing. What do you feel literature can do for technology and vice versa?
I would reframe the question slightly, because technology and literature have been fused together from the beginning of both. Books themselves are a technology – a hugely successful one – and so the emergence of things like tablets and e-readers is less a grand reckoning and more an interesting development in a long-running saga. We only have the literature we have today because of technology. Or, to put it another way: technology is no stranger to the bookshop.

4. Besides Mr. Penumbra's 24-hour Bookstore, which is your favourite bookshop?
I have two hometown favourites: one is City Light Books, long a San Francisco institution, and the other is Green Apple Books, which used to be my neighbourhood bookstore out in the city's foggy Richmond District. I used to stalk Green Apple's shelves in the evenings and dream of having a book there myself someday.

5. What would your bookshop of the future look like?
I don't think it looks that different from the very best bookstores of the present – but that's the key, isn't it? The very best. The great bookstores of 2014 do more than sell books;

they serve as public spaces and gathering places. They organize events and convene conversations. In short, their shelves and their stock are only the beginning of what they have to offer, and that will only become more true as time goes on.

6. What is your favourite typeface?

Oh, it changes day by day, but at the moment, I'm in love with Eskapade Fraktur, a modern blackletter designed by Veronika Burian and José Scaglione. I'm using it on my website.

7. Who would win in a fight, Ernest Hemingway or Mark Zuckerberg?

Who says they have to fight? They should get a drink. I'm sure each could learn a thing or two from the other.

A NOTE ON THE AUTHOR

Robin Sloan grew up near Detroit and has worked at Poynter, Current TV and Twitter in jobs that have generally had 'something to do with figuring out the future of media'. His first novel, *Mr Penumbra's 24-Hour Bookstore*, was an international bestseller. He lives in San Francisco.